NORTHBROOK PUBLIC LIBRARY
1201 CEDAR LANE
NORTHBROOK, ILL 60062

FEB 1 1 2014

Northbrook Public Library

3 1123 01055 3892

P9-CEH-963

CAPTAIN AWESOME

GETS CRUSHED

By STAN KIRBY

Illustrated by GEORGE O'CONNOR

LITTLE SIMON

New York   London   Toronto   Sydney   New Delhi

If you purchased this book without a cover, you should be aware that this book is stolen property. It was reported as "unsold and destroyed" to the publisher, and neither the author nor the publisher has received any payment for this "stripped book."

This book is a work of fiction. Any references to historical events, real people, or real places are used fictitiously. Other names, characters, places, and events are products of the author's imagination, and any resemblance to actual events or places or persons, living or dead, is entirely coincidental.

LITTLE SIMON

An imprint of Simon & Schuster Children's Publishing Division • 1230 Avenue of the Americas, New York, New York 10020 • Copyright © 2013 by Simon & Schuster, Inc. All rights reserved, including the right of reproduction in whole or in part in any form. LITTLE SIMON is a registered trademark of Simon & Schuster, Inc., and associated colophon is a trademark of Simon & Schuster, Inc. For information about special discounts for bulk purchases, please contact Simon & Schuster Special Sales at 1-866-506-1949 or business@simonandschuster.com. The Simon & Schuster Speakers Bureau can bring authors to your live event. For more information or to book an event contact the Simon & Schuster Speakers Bureau at 1-866-248-3049 or visit our website at www.simonspeakers.com. Designed by Jay Colvin. Manufactured in the United States of America 1113 FFG First Edition 10 9 8 7 6 5 4 3 2 1

Kirby, Stan. Captain Awesome gets crushed / by Stan Kirby ; illustrated by George O'Connor. — 1st ed. p. cm. — (Captain Awesome ; #9) Summary: Captain Awesome (otherwise known as Eugene McGillicudy) faces his latest challenge—making it through Valentine's Day at school while trying to find out the identity of his secret admirer. 1. Superheroes—Juvenile fiction. 2. Valentine's Day—Juvenile fiction. 3. Schools—Juvenile fiction. [1. Superheroes—Fiction. 2. Valentine's Day—Fiction. 3. Schools—Fiction.] I. O'Connor, George, ill. II. Title. III. Series: Kirby, Stan. Captain Awesome ; no. 9. PZ7.K633529Cagm 2013 813.6—dc23 2012038755

ISBN 978-1-4424-8212-8 (pbk)

ISBN 978-1-4424-8213-5 (hc)

ISBN 978-1-4424-8214-2 (eBook)

Table of Contents

1. Comic Book Day of Destiny!....................... 1

2. An Evil Surprise.. 17

3. Don't Stare at the Pink!........................... 29

4. Valentines of Icy Doom............................. 45

5. The Secret of the Secret Admirer's
Secrets.. 55

6. Beware His Stinky Seaweeder!................. 73

7. Double Secret Coolness!............................ 83

8. The Mystery of the Missing
Cupcake of Yumminess.............................. 91

9. The Great Anonymous Super Dude Fan 103

CHAPTER 1

Comic Book
Day of Destiny!

By
Eugene

Run!

"Hurry up, Charlie!" Eugene McGillicudy urged his best friend. Charlie Thomas Jones rushed to keep up, but Eugene was moving superfast.

It was a big day! Eugene ran through the Sunnyview Mall. His feet thudded against the marble floor. His heart raced. He could smell the new comic books like a hungry dog smells bacon.

YUM!

This was all because today was **New Comic Book Day!**

I love the sound of that, Eugene thought. Then he thought it again.

New Comic Book Day!

It was the greatest day ever for Eugene, Charlie, and all comic book fans—the day when all the new comic books for the week came out. It was like Christmas, wrapped up in a birthday, sitting in a bucket of Halloween candy.

"Come on, Charlie!" Eugene

called. "We don't want to miss the new comics!"

Charlie's backpack bounced against his back.

BOING! BOING! BOING!

Eugene saw Super Superhero Superstore just ahead and ran even faster. With each step, Eugene thought of the treasures that waited for him on the shelves. What would the new issue of Super Dude con-tain? Would there be a *Super Dude Winter Annual of Goodness vs. Evil?* Or maybe a *Super Dude February Spectacular?*

What's that you say?

WHO IS SUPER DUDE?

Can it be that you've never

heard of him? Is such a thing even possible?! Do you live in a world without comic books and TV shows and movies and all the awesome stuff that makes life awesome?

Super Dude is the world's greatest superhero—even gooder than the Incredible Good Guy and even smackier than Captain Smackdown. Super Dude is the superhero who once punched out the power-draining lights of the Fluorescent Freaky

Freak and tackled the Soccerbull before he scored his evil goal of destruction.

But Super Dude was more to Eugene than just the greatest hero of all time. He was the reason Eugene became Sunnyview's first and most awesome superhero. Secretly, you see, Eugene was the one, the only . . .

CAPTAIN AWESOME!

MI-TEE!

That's right. Sunnyview had its very own superhero!

And not just one, either.

With his best friend, Charlie (also known as Nacho Cheese Man), and their class's pet hamster, Turbo, Eugene formed the Sunnyview Superhero Squad to stop the eviling of bad guys and to keep Sunnyview safe.

"Safety first!" That was the first rule of the Sunnyview Superhero Squad. And the second rule was "Buy new comic books every

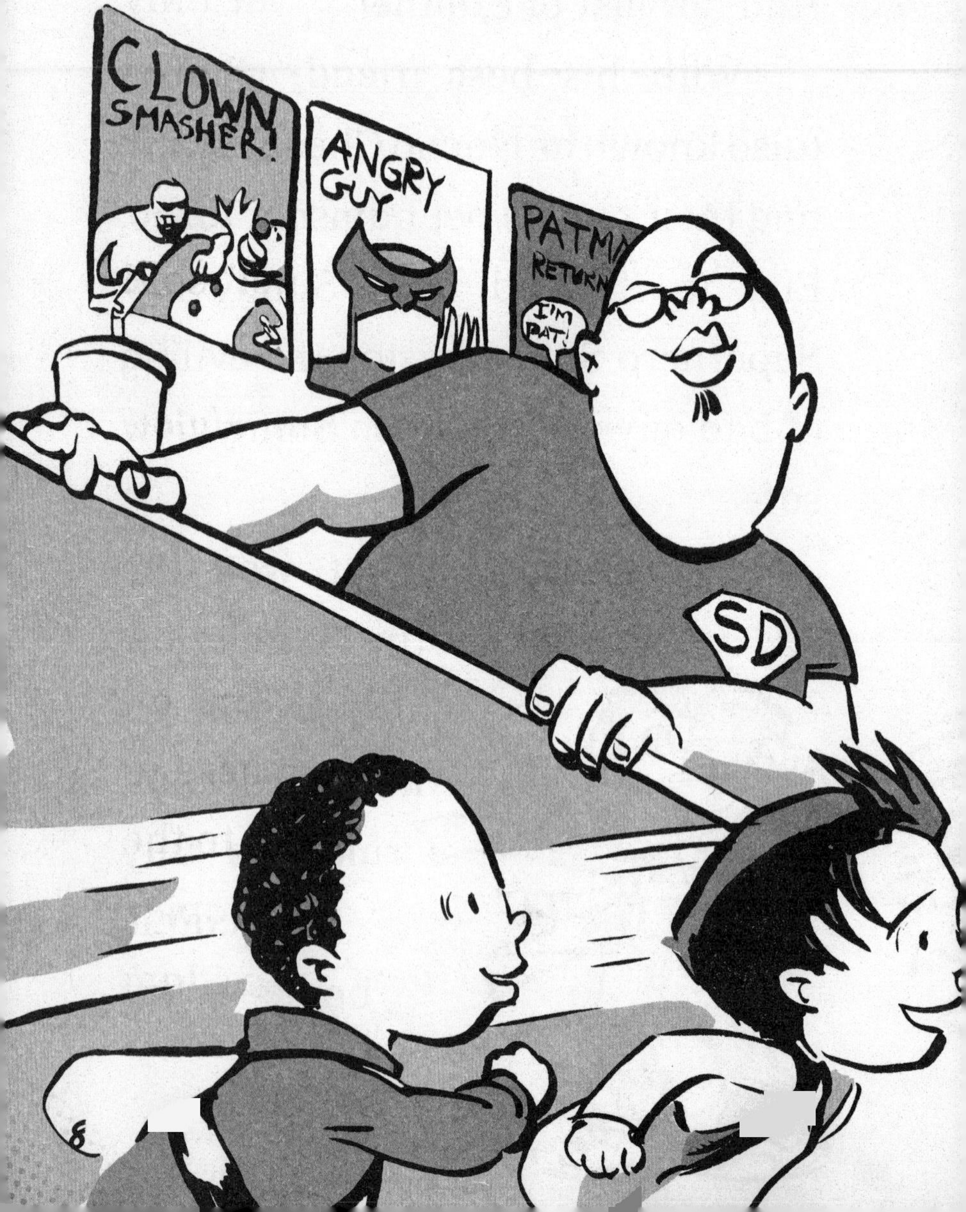
CLOWN SMASHER!
ANGRY GUY
PATM
RETURN
I'M PAT!
SD

New Comic Book Day"—but only if they starred Super Dude or any of the Legion of Super Duders or the Super Dude Family.

"Good morning, Eugene!" said Biggie Ulm, the big guy behind the counter. "How's my favorite super-hero?"

"Morning, Biggie! How's my favorite comic book store?"

Eugene didn't wait for an answer. He knew exactly where to go. He raced past the counter to the comic book rack. He passed copies of Beach Bummer: The Caped Clam

Fighter No. 23, Clown Smasher No. 9, and Space Shuttle Romance No. 15. And then he saw it: the new issue of Super Dude. It was No. 384, with Super Dude delivering his one-two superslap in a story called *The Pulse-Pounding Punch Out of Pecos Pepper.*

Eugene grabbed the last two copies and handed one to Charlie.

Charlie held his copy to his nose and sniffed. "Ahhhhhh. Still has that new comic smell!"

WHEW!

Mission accomplished!

"Too bad you didn't get here sooner," Biggie said. "You could

have had the last copy of *Super
Dude Super Duper Spectacular
Winter Extra Special* No. 1."

Eugene's eyes widened and his
jaw dropped. "It—it's gone?"

"I sold my last copy to a girl who was in here just five minutes ago," Biggie told the boys.

A GIRL? Reading an issue of Super Dude?

Only two words described what Eugene was thinking: NON and SENSE. Someone wanted to keep him from having that comic book.

This could only be the work of the evil **Collector Queen**! Her job was to take comic

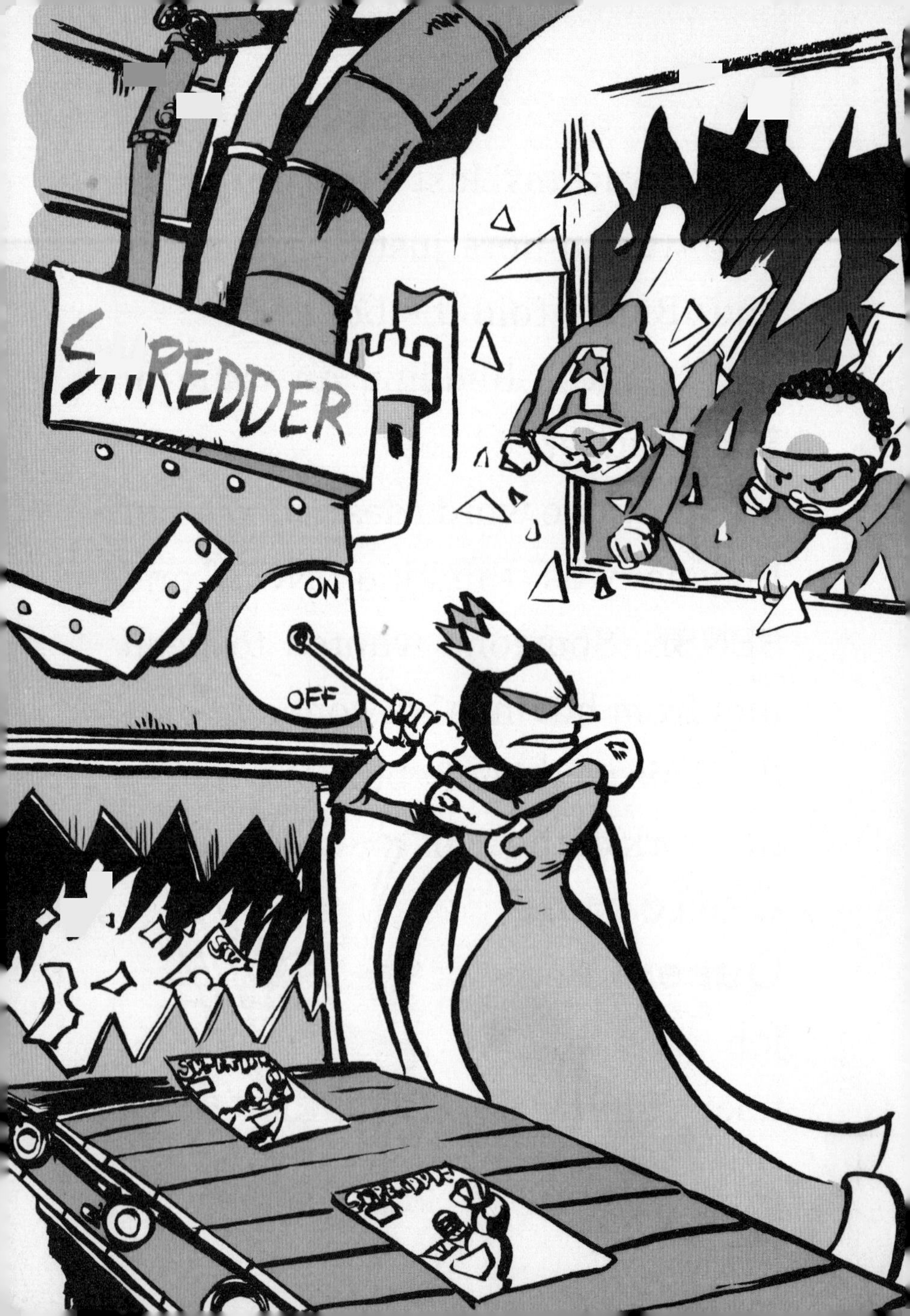
ON
OFF

books from the hands of young boys and shred them in her evil Shredding Palace of Paper Strips so no one could ever, ever, EVER read the adventures of Super Dude!

EVER!

"Come on, Charlie!" Captain Awesome said in his most heroic voice. "We've got a comic book thief to take care of! MI-TEE!"

"Right behind you, Captain!" Then Charlie opened his backpack and took out a spray can of taco-flavored nacho cheese. "I'm ready for action!"

CHAPTER 2

An Evil Surprise

By
Eugene

Now Eugene knew how Super Dude felt in Super Dude No. 91, the issue where Super Dude lost his powers and was just called Mister Dude.

TERRIBLE!

Until today, Eugene had never missed an issue of Super Dude or any of the Specials, Annuals, or Spectaculars.

"Oh, cheer up, Eugene," Charlie

said. "Maybe we can order a copy online."

"That will take for-EVER!" Eugene said. "At least a couple of days!" Eugene's head slumped, his shoulders sagged with sadness, and even his shoes sounded unhappy as they flopped on the mall floor.

GASP!

Charlie stopped and stared. Eugene crashed into him.

"What is it, Charlie?"

"Red alert, Eugene!" he cried. "I

mean Pink! *Pink* alert!" Charlie's eyes practically bugged out of his head.

Eugene looked around the mall. That's when he saw it. He'd been too distracted racing to the comic book store to notice it sooner.

NO! His brain nearly exploded!

The color pink was everywhere. Ribbons, hearts, sparkly paper snowflakes, stars, and flowers were on every door and window and bench. And they were all pink.

Eugene was surrounded by it. **PINK! GAK!**

It was like someone ate too much cotton candy and barfed it all over the mall.

Jumbled Juice sold pink slushies in pink cups. Trendy Treads had a display of pink sneakers and pink boots. Even Dr. Pugh Pilz, Sunnyview's one-eyed eye doctor, had a pair of giant pink sunglasses hanging in his window.

Pink was one of Captain Awesome's weaknesses. Not as powerful as fried okra or an asparagus spear, but it could still weaken him and drain his powers.

"I've got pink madness!" Eugene cried. His arms felt heavy at his side. His knees wobbled like wet

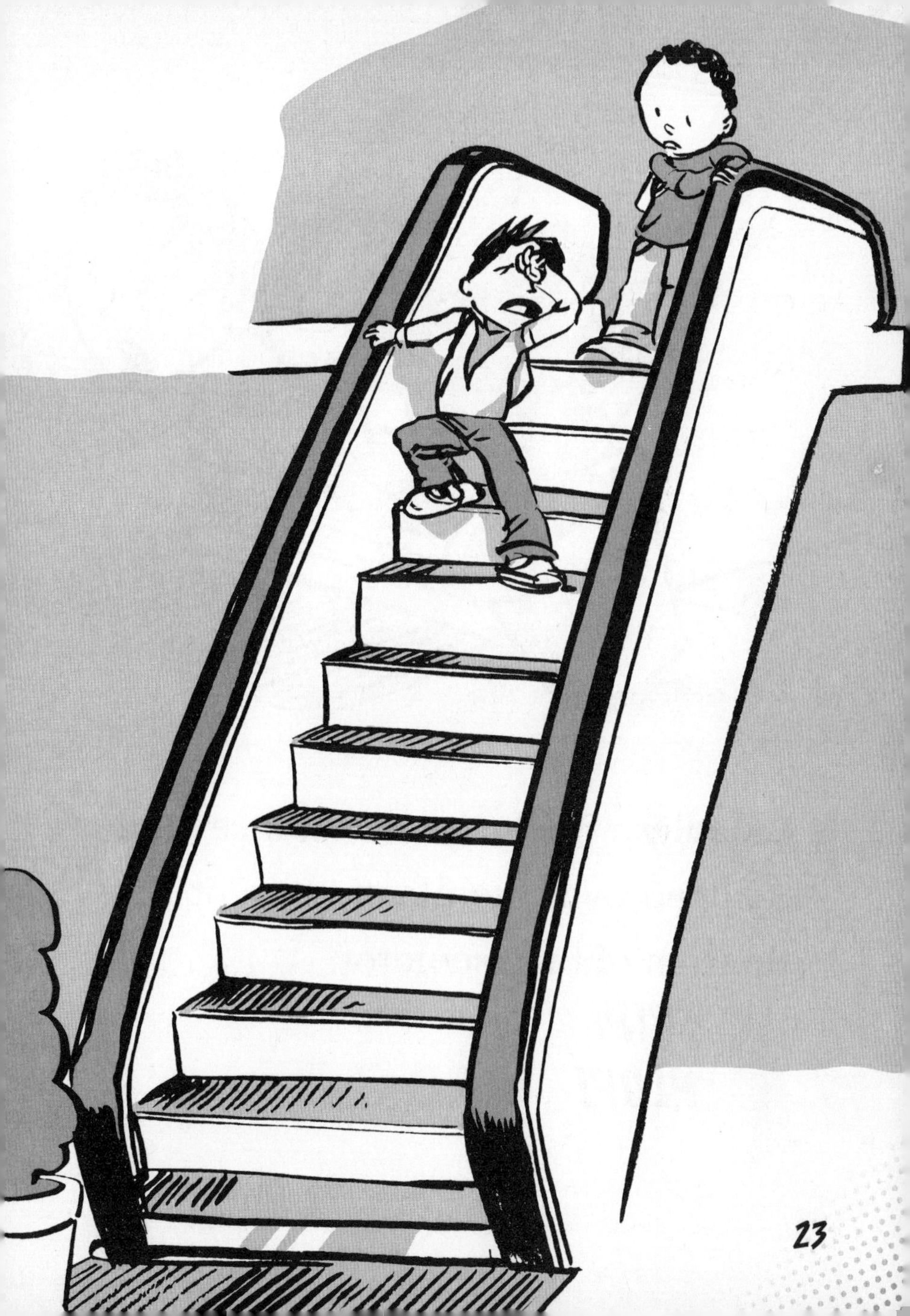

noodles. He lost his balance and tripped over the plastic tree at the bottom of the escalator.

TRIP!

PLOP!

Eugene was weak as he tried to stand. It was as if some pink villain was taking all the powers from his body.

Who did this to me? he thought. *Who?*

Suddenly someone helped him to his feet. "Happy Valentine's Day, Eugene!" It was Eugene's neighbor and classmate Sally Williams.

Valentine's Day! Of course! Eugene thought. "Hi, Sally. Thanks," he said.

"Hi, Sally," Charlie repeated.

"I just finished my Valentine's Day shopping." She held up a big

shopping bag. "I think I've got every-thing I need. Did you guys pick out your valentines yet? Only a couple of days before the big day! See ya!"

Then she breezed down the mall and disappeared into Stuffy's Toy-O-Rama, which was filled with fuzzy pink stuffed rabbits and even pinker teddy bears.

CHAPTER 3

Don't Stare at the Pink!

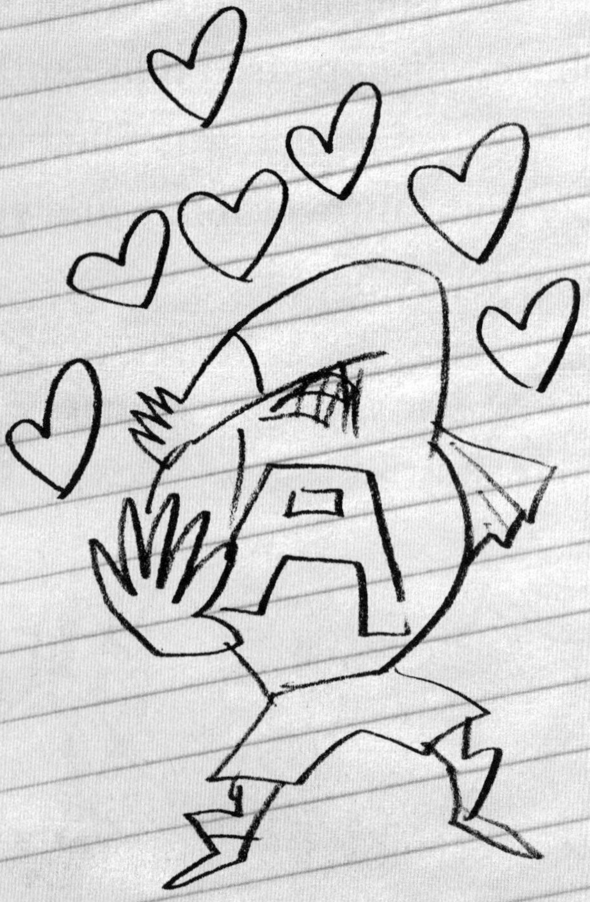

By Eugene

Eugene and Charlie walked to school together every day, unless it was one of three days.

1. Sick Day
2. Holiday
3. Saving the World from Evil Day

Today was not any of those days, so Eugene and Charlie headed to school. They were just a few feet from the front door when Eugene's arm started shaking.

SHAKE!

His eye?

TWITCH!

His nose?

SCRINCH!

Eugene knew what was going on. His Cootie Sense was tingling.

COOTIES WERE IN THE AIR!

That's when Eugene heard the voice that turned his feet to stone. He and Charlie froze on the sidewalk.

"Oh, look! It's Barf-gene and his best friend. Hi, Charlie."

Eugene always knew that horrible screech of a voice. It was worse than his mom telling him to turn off the TV and get ready for bed.

It was Meredith Mooney, the

pinkest girl in the whole school.

She was dressed head to toe and back to head again in pink— pink ribbons in her hair, pink polish on her fingernails, and pink shoes with matching pink socks.

This wasn't for Valentine's Day, though. Meredith dressed like this *every* day.

"Aren't you going to wish me a happy Valentine's Day, Dumb-gene?"

"Ugh! ME! MY! MERE-DITH!" Eugene said. "Happy day *before* Valentine's Day."

"I like to celebrate the day before, the day of, *and* the day after," Meredith said. "It's *all* so pink and wonderful!"

She said the last part like it was a song. A sick, awful song that made Eugene's stomach hurt as if he'd drunk an okra-and-beet milk shake.

Valentine's Day was like that. Every year on February 14, boys and girls passed around little paper cards filled with hearts and swirly pictures of the second most evil baby in the world, Cupid (after Queen Stinkypants, Eugene's little sister from Planet Baby).

But what good was it? Did you get presents like at Christmas or

your birthday? Did you get to dress up like at Halloween? Or eat tons of food like at Thanksgiving? No, no, and no again.

Valentine's Day was a day of gross girly colors like lavender and red . . . and *pink*!

"Good-bye, Dull-gene! See you, Charlie!" Meredith hurried into school. "Don't be late for class."

Class! But of course! Eugene thought.

The Sunnyview Mall may have been taken over by the pink craziness of Valentine's Day, but they'd be safe from it once they got into the school building.

"We'll be okay inside, Charlie," Eugene said.

"I hope you're right," Charlie replied.

But he wasn't.

Inside the school, Eugene felt as if he'd been blasted by an icy blast of the Icy Blaster's Ice Blaster. His eyes were as wide as plates and his mouth fell open like the draw-bridge of a castle.

"Haaaaappy Valentine's Day, Eugene!"

"Haaaaappy Valentine's Day, Charlie!"

"Haaaaappy Valentine's Day, Eugene and Charlie!"

Everybody was saying it. The pink madness of Valentine's Day had infected the school.

Classroom doors had little pink heart stickers stuck to them. Bathrooms had red construction paper hearts taped up. Swirls of pink and red streamers twisted from the ceiling.

"Happy Valentine's Day!"

Can't anybody say "Hi" or "Good morning" anymore? Eugene thought.

And that's when it struck Eugene like a bolt of lightning. Not the kind of lightning that started fires or split trees, but the kind that gave someone super lightning powers.

This was *her* fault. This was *her* evil pink and gross brainwashing plan.

My! Me! Mine! Meredith's!

Meredith Mooney was way

more than the girl in Eugene's class who bothered him and wore too much pink. She was really Captain Awesome's evil enemy, Little Miss Stinky Pinky!

"This is the work of *her*," said Captain Awesome.

"You mean Little Miss Stinky

Pinky?" Charlie wondered aloud.

"Exactly," Eugene said. His eyes narrowed.

"Cheesy-yoooo." Nacho Cheese Man let out a low whistle.

"And she's covered our world with her pink evil, turning it into a Pink Palace of Doom!" Captain Awesome said in his loudest and

most awesome hero voice. "This is a job for Captain Awesome!"

"And Nacho Cheese Man!" cried his best friend in his cheesiest hero voice.

CHAPTER 4

Valentines of Icy Doom

By Eugene

Eugene and Charlie made it to
their classroom in plenty of time.
And there was a surprise waiting
for them in their cubbies.

"DON'T TOUCH IT!"

Charlie was reaching for the
envelope when Eugene screamed
out his warning.

"Freeze, Charlie! And whatever
you do, don't open that envelope."

Charlie held the envelope away

from his body like it was his mother's purse.

"Why? What's wrong, Eugene?" Charlie said. "Is it evil paper with deadly ink?"

"Worse. Charlie, do you remember Mr. Freezer?"

Charlie unfroze and dropped the envelope on the floor.

"That's right!" Charlie said. "He used to send us notes too. Evil notes of evil."

What is it about cold weather that makes bad guys want to write notes? They should be busy making hot chocolate, but they always find time to write down some evil.

RIIIIP!

Eugene carefully opened his envelope. He shook it. Nothing fell out. No bomb, no booby trap, no rattlesnake.

Not even a paper cut.

WHEW!

Eugene stuck his fingers inside
and pulled out a slip of
paper. It was not a fro-
zen message of icy doom
from Mr. Freezer.

It was a drawing of
Captain Awesome.

"Wow, that looks
just like you!" Charlie
exclaimed. "Let's see what I got!"

Charlie opened his envelope
and slid out a piece of paper. "It's
blank! I got nothing!"

their names. Who could have done this?

The only ones who know our secret identities are Turbo and Sally, Eugene thought.

Eugene shot a glance at Turbo. The class hamster squeaked happily on his exercise wheel. He didn't do it. He couldn't even hold a pencil.

"Try turning it over," Eugene suggested.

Charlie flipped the paper, revealing a drawing of Nacho Cheese Man. "Looks just like me, too! *Just* like me!"

Eugene shook his head. This didn't make sense. "Someone is sending us a message, Charlie. But I don't know what it is."

"I do!" Charlie shouted. "Some-one really likes to draw!"

"And someone also knows that we're secretly Captain Awesome and Nacho Cheese Man, Charlie," Eugene said. "But who?"

"Someone who really likes to draw!" Charlie repeated, holding his drawing. "Look at how they cap-tured the wonder of my cheese pow-ers with just a pencil. It's cheese-tastic!"

Eugene looked at the drawing carefully. There was no signature and nothing on the envelope but

Eugene looked at Sally. She was busy at her desk, getting ready for class to start.

Sally would never leave me a special note. Would she?

Eugene's mind raced faster than Super Dude's friend, Speedy Speedman. Who was leaving them secret messages? Who else knew their secret identities? What was going on?

CHAPTER 5

The Secret of the Secret Admirer's Secrets

By
Eugene

BLECH!

Eugene looked down at his lunch tray. Something that looked like meat was next to something that looked like tree bark that was next to something wiggly that looked like it was going to jump out of the tray, chase him around the cafeteria, and try to bite him on the ear.

But before its hungry tentacles

could whip around his neck, Eugene grabbed it and tossed it into the trash.

Eugene sped away from the trash can and sat down next to Charlie in their special Sunnyview Superhero Squad seats. The seats were special because of one thing:

1. From them, you could see all the doors and windows in the cafeteria, so if any supervillain tried anything villainous, the superheroes would be ready.

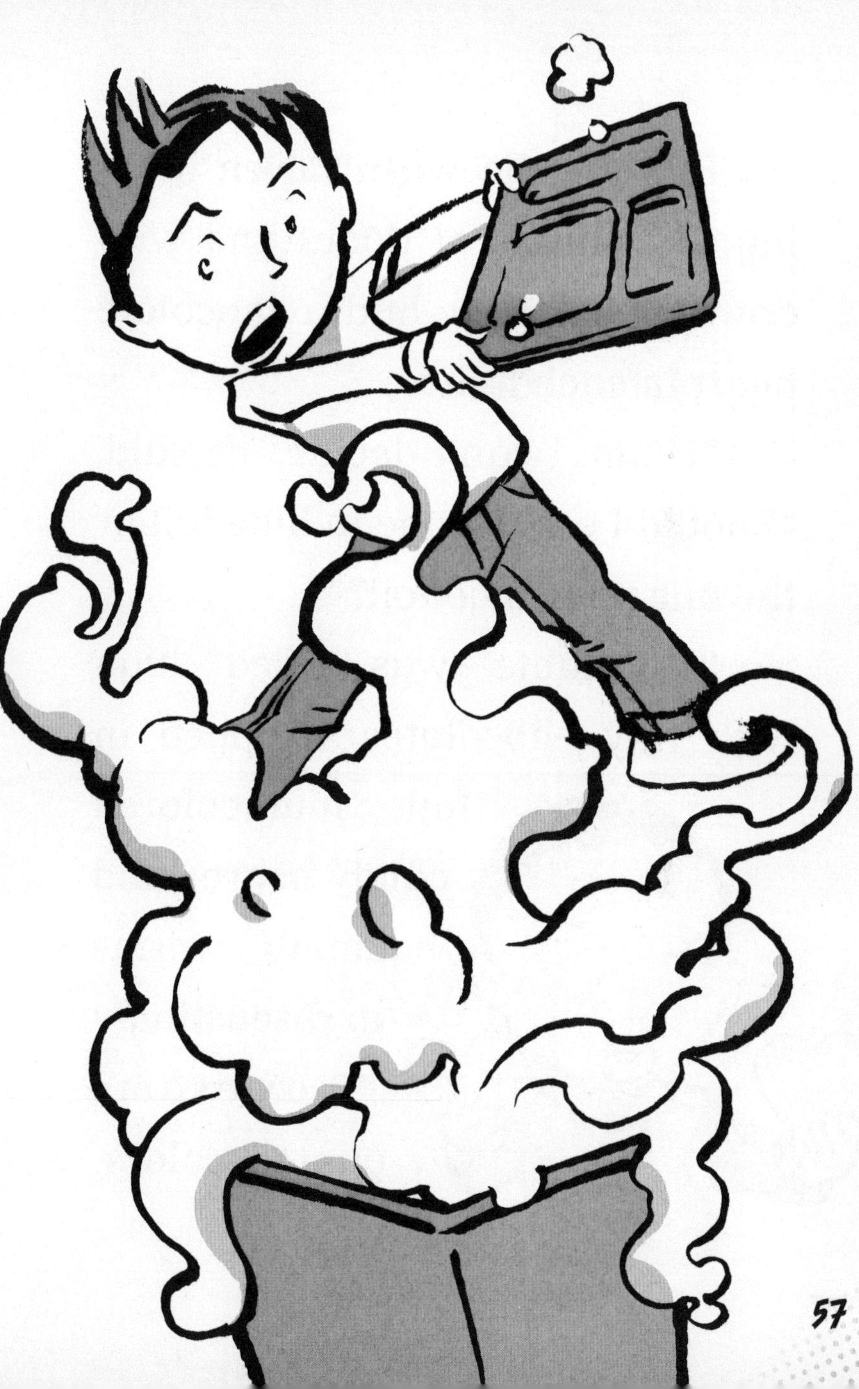

But Charlie wasn't even looking for villains at doors and windows. Because he had a chocolate heart in each hand.

"Hmm. I can't decide," he said. "Should I eat the one in blue foil or the one in orange foil?"

The table was piled high with tiny chocolates wrapped in foil, multicolored candy hearts, and gummy worms in disgustingly awesome gummy colors.

"Where did all this stuff come from?" Eugene asked.

"They're gifts from my Valentine," Charlie said happily.

Gifts? From a—WAIT! WHAT? A valentine? Eugene's head was swirling. "You mean Dr. Varney Valentine, right? The evil maker of evil stuffed unicorns that are stuffed with evil?"

Charlie shook his head. He pointed across the cafeteria to

where a girl all dressed in pink was sitting.

"MY-ME-ME-MEREDITH MOONEY?!" Eugene could barely spit out the words.

Meredith waved at Charlie and smiled. She looked at Eugene and stuck out her tongue.

"Guess she's kind of got a crush on me," Charlie said.

"*Meredith Mooney?*" Eugene repeated.

"Yup. She wants me to be her Valentine," Charlie said.

"But it's Meredith! Mooney!" Eugene cried.

"Nothing wrong with feeling special, Eugene," Charlie said. "And the best part? Free candy." Charlie picked up a gummy worm, squirted a small blast of jalapeno cheese on it, and pressed another gummy worm on top. "Mmmmm, gummies and cheese!"

If there was one thing Charlie

loved more than cheese from a can, it was free candy.

"B-but Charlie! This is My! Me! Mine! Meredith! She's not just annoying and gross, she's the arch-enemy of the Sunnyview Superhero Squad! *We're* the Sunnyview Super-hero Squad and *she's* Little Miss Stinky Pinky."

"And now I'm her Valentine," Charlie said, preparing another gummy sandwich.

Eugene plopped into his seat. "She's up to something, Charlie, and that something is no good! Maybe she's just playing nice for Valentine's Day."

"I'm not the only one, though," Charlie said.

"Sally's got a Valentine too, but he's a secret. Look."

Eugene looked.

Sally had a giant heart-shaped box of candy in front of her. Eugene waved, but she was too busy opening a card to see him.

"No!" Eugene cried. "This is bad news for the Sunnyview Superhero Squad!"

"Why? Do you think Chunky Chuck gave us explosive chocolate?" Charlie asked.

"Worse. If Beastosaurus, the Sea Beast from the Deepest Deep climbed out of the ocean and started stomping on houses and cars, we'd need our whole team to push him back into the water." That meant Captain Awesome, Nacho Cheese Man, Turbo, *and*

Supersonic Sal, the girl who was now eating a chocolate-covered cherry and *not* looking at Eugene.

"Don't worry, Eugene. Tomorrow is Valentine's Day. You've still got plenty of time to get your own Valentine," Charlie told him.

Plenty of time, Eugene thought. *Sure, like Beastosaurus will be happy to wait around before he*

launches his Beastostompo attack.

"Who's Sally's secret Valentine?" Eugene wondered aloud as he scanned the cafeteria.

Suddenly Eugene leaped to his feet.

"Supergasp!" he cried. "I bet Sally's secret admirer is really Beastosaurus! This valentine junk is really his fiendish plot to distract the Sunnyview Superhero Squad while he attacks!"

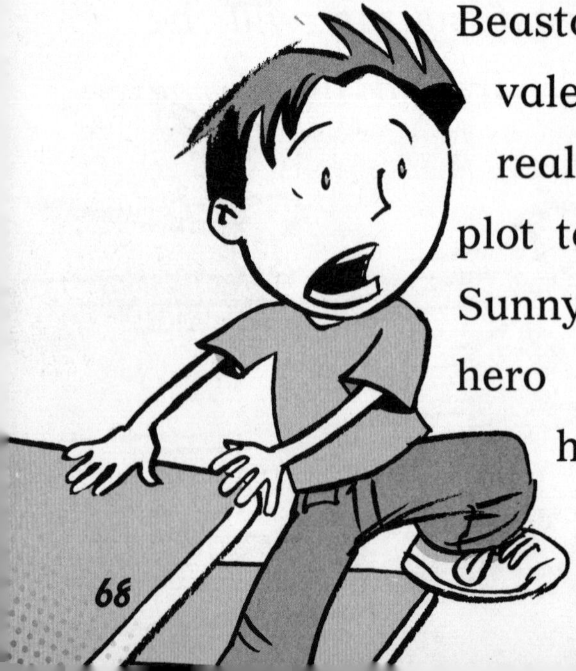

"Well, next time, I hope he comes up with a distraction that has more caramel in it," Charlie replied, popping a piece of chocolate into his mouth. "Besides, what do you care who Sally's secret Valentine is?" Charlie asked.

"I don't care," Eugene blurted out. "I don't care at all. Why should I care? I laugh at you. HA!"

"For someone who doesn't care, you sure seem to care," said Charlie.

Eugene slumped. Charlie had free candy. Sally had a secret admirer. All Eugene had was a pile of something that might be green peas on his lunch tray. Now Eugene knew exactly how Super Dude felt in Super Dude No. 14 when Mr. Floss stole all of Super Dude's secret candy stash from the Super Dude Hall of Dessertness and replaced it with lima beans.

How come Charlie can't see the danger in it all! Eugene wondered. *Pink and red hearts! Hugs! Secret admirers! Could there be anything more evil than that?! Or yucky?!*

Eugene knew that this time Captain Awesome would have to go it alone!

CHAPTER 6

Beware His Stinky Seaweeder!

By Eugene

Eugene raced from the cafeteria, put on his Captain Awesome outfit, and raced back as quickly as possible.

"Citizens! Drop that candy! Put down those Valentine's Day cards! And whatever you do, flee from the pink hearts!" Captain Awesome called out. "It's all a wicked plot of the dreaded Beastosaurus! Beware his stinky seaweeder!"

Captain Awesome jumped onto a table and pulled down the pink streamers that hung overhead. "Take that, you dreaded pink tentacles of romance!"

The streamers trailed from behind Captain Awesome as he

jumped onto another table where Meredith was eating her lunch.

"You're getting streamers in my pudding!" Meredith yelled at him.

"Someday, you'll thank me for that!" Captain Awesome said and pulled down another set of pink streamers stretched over the table.

Captain Awesome was about to jump down and race over to the big red and pink hearts, but as

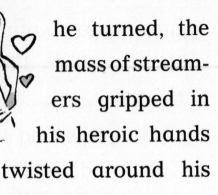

he turned, the mass of stream-ers gripped in his heroic hands twisted around his legs, making it difficult to move.

"You won't stop me, you horrible holiday decoration!" Captain Awe-some declared. Then he added, in a much less heroic voice, "Or maybe you will," as he fell off the table with a . . .

SUPERTHUD!

Captain Awesome squirmed on the ground, trying to break free from the streamers of doom.

Charlie rushed over, yanked them off Captain Awesome's legs, and helped the superhero sit up.

"Thanks, Nacho Cheese Man," Captain Awesome whispered to Charlie, so no one would know his secret superhero identity.

The once nicely decorated

cafeteria was a mess. Kids looked around, not sure what to make of it all. And Meredith Mooney fumed as she picked little bits of pink paper from her pudding.

"Here. Have some Valentine's candy," Charlie said as he offered Captain Awesome a candy heart. "I'm sure you'll get some of your own tomorrow."

"I don't want any candy. What

makes you think I want candy?"
Captain Awesome said defensively.
"And why do you keep saying that I
care about Sally having a secret
admirer? 'Cause I *don't*."

"But I didn't say anything about
that," Charlie replied, confused.

"But you *wanted* to. I can tell.
I'm a superhero. It's one of my powers," Captain Awesome said. "In
fact, I'm *happy* I don't have any

candy or a Valentine card from Sally—I mean *someone*. There's no room in my backpack for all that stuff. And who'd want to be part of a holiday that brainwashes everyone into liking pink?! And believe me, I *do not* care who Sally's secret admirer is. I just want to find out because . . . because . . . it could be the Secret Admir-inator! Yeah! Sent from the future to pretend to be Sally's secret admirer!"

"But I thought you said it was Beastosaurus," Charlie said.

"I changed my mind," Captain Awesome said in a huff.

Captain Awesome and Charlie stared at each other in silence for a moment before Charlie finally said, "I think all this pink is turning your brain to mush."

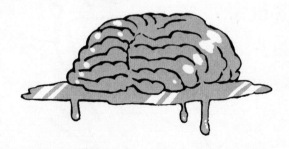

CHAPTER 7

Double Secret Coolness!

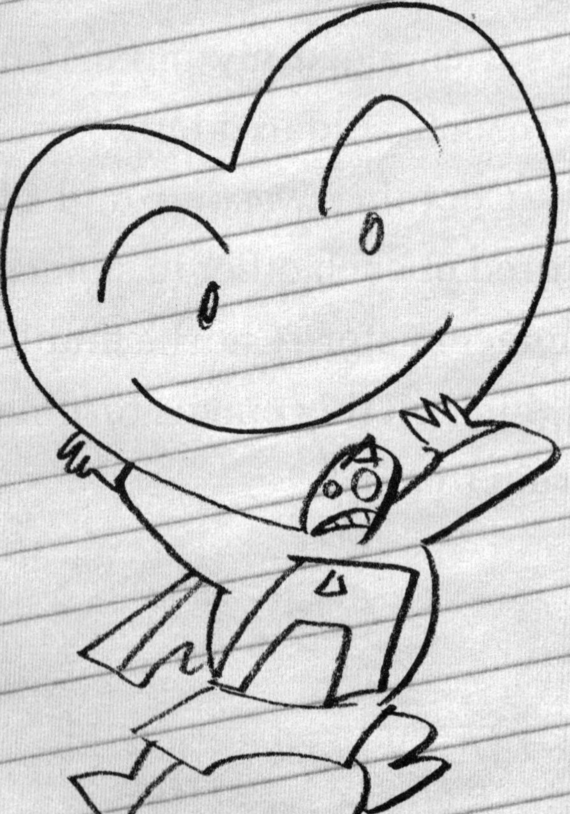

By Eugene

Valentine's Day finally arrived and that could only mean one thing. **BARF!**

Eugene was dreading this day even more than a first day back to school after getting a haircut. "What happened? Get in a fight with a lawnmower?" was the only thing he had to suffer through on those haircut days. This day was going to be a bajillion times worse.

Eugene was going to be the first kid in the history of history to not receive a valentine on Valentine's Day. Even when Valentine's Day was first invented by cavemen, all the cave kids in dinoschool still received a rock chiseled into the shape of heart.

"All right, class, is everyone ready for our Valentine's Day party? Who wants a cupcake?" Eugene's teacher Ms. Beasley asked.

As the rest of the kids in class cheered, Eugene opened his math notebook. That's when he saw . . . **IT!**

Tucked between the pages of his notebook was a blue, red, and yellow note! Eugene eagerly opened it. It was decorated with stars and Super Dude stickers.

CHEER!

IT WAS A VALENTINE! Yes, it was a one-hundred-percent Eugene's-not-the-only-kid-in-the-history-of-history-to-not-receive-a-valentine valentine! The note had eleven simple words that sent Eugene's spirits flying: "Happy Valentine's Day to my favorite superhero! Look in your cubby."

"Mi-tee," Eugene whispered to himself, not only because he had a secret admirer, but because there wasn't a single dot of pink on the whole card.

Eugene was about to smile, but then the most horrible thought in all the multidimensions of horrible thoughts exploded into his head like an overinflated birthday cake. He thrust the card out to Charlie, whose cheek was stuffed with chalky candy hearts like he was a sugar-crazy chipmunk.

"Is this from you?!" Eugene asked.

"Mut? *Mo!* My midn't mive moo mat," Charlie mumbled.

"Are you sure?" Eugene asked.

"Mes mime mur," Charlie replied.

Eugene plopped back into his chair with a huge sigh of relief.

Eugene had a secret admirer!

And even better, he had a secret admirer who liked Super Dude!

DOUBLE SECRET COOLNESS!

Maybe this whole Valentine's Day thing isn't so gross after all, Eugene thought. *Now . . . how do I get to my cubby without anyone noticing?*

CHAPTER 8

The Mystery of the Missing Cupcake of Yumminess

By Eugene

As Eugene crawled along the floor to his cubby, he pulled out his Valentine's Day card one more time. "Happy Valentine's Day to my favorite superhero!" it read. Eugene smiled.

Then he saw . . . another **IT!**

A copy of *Super Dude Super Duper Spectacular Winter Extra Special* No. 1!

IN. HIS. CUBBY!

He grabbed it and almost started to dance with joy, but just then he saw Sally peeking out from around the other cubbies. She smiled as Eugene hugged the comic to his chest.

The moment Eugene noticed her, Sally's eyes went wide and she began to fumble through the backpacks.

"What are you doing, Sally?" Eugene asked.

"Um, nothing. Just looking for my backpack," Sally replied. "Oh! Look! Here it is!" Sally grabbed a backpack and held it out.

"That's Jake's," Eugene said.

"Oh, right. So it is." Sally blushed. She dropped the backpack and scurried back to her chair.

Despite all the ickiness of Valentine's Day, Eugene was feeling pretty good because of three things:

1. Secret Admirer
2. Cupcakes
3. New Super Dude comic book

As Eugene returned to his seat, he looked at Charlie. "Life is good," he said.

"You got that right," Charlie replied. "Although I kind of wish Meredith would stop smiling at me. It's really weirding me out."

"Sally is acting kind of strange too," Eugene added.

"Maybe all the girls in our class got bitten by the Lovebuggerinator," Charlie said.

Eugene nodded and leaned back in his chair. All that was left for him to do was sit back and enjoy the cupcake Mrs. Beasley had given him. Sure, it was pink with red frosting, but that was the great thing about cupcakes. No matter their color, they were still awesome.

And then suddenly . . . his cupcake was gone! Eugene quickly pulled Charlie over to the cubbies.

"I dare say that evil is eviling in

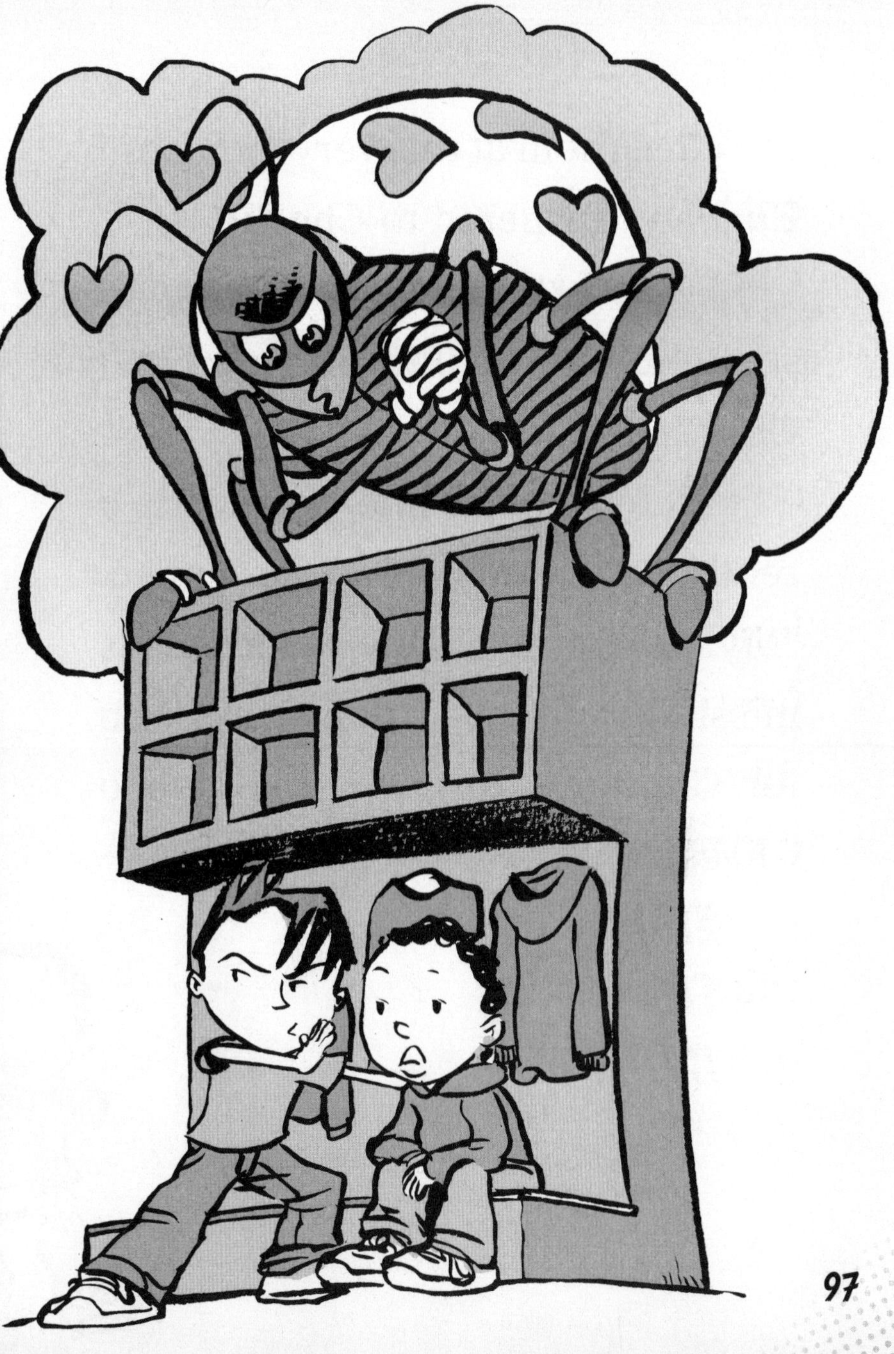

our classroom at this very moment!" Eugene whispered to Charlie.

"Where?! I always wanted to see what evil eviling looked like!" Charlie replied.

"It looks just like ugly with a really bad haircut," Eugene replied. "My Valentine's Day cupcake is missing! And this is definitely a job for Captain Awesome and Nacho Cheese Man!"

ZIP!
TIE!
CAPE!

In a burst and a flash, Eugene McGillicudy and Charlie Thomas Jones transformed into the terrific twosome, Captain Awesome and Nacho Cheese Man!

With the cry of "MI-TEE!" and "CHEESY YO!" Captain Awesome and Nacho Cheese Man charged into the middle of the classroom.

"Captain Awesome and . . . was it Cheddar Cheese Man?" Ms. Beasley asked. "So nice of you to join our little Valentine's Day party."

"It's *Nacho* Cheese Man, ma'am," Nacho Cheese Man told her. "I'm saving the world with canned cheese!"

"We're here to solve the mystery of the Missing Cupcake of Yumminess!" added

Captain Awesome.

"I didn't even know there was a Cupcake of Yumminess or that it was missing," Ms. Beasley replied.

"There is!" Captain Awesome said. "And it's really, really yummy!"

But before Captain Awesome could say even another word, Supersonic Sal joined them in the middle of the class. She directed Meredith into the middle as well. Meredith clenched a cupcake in her hand.

CHAPTER 9

The Great Anonymous Super Dude Fan

By
Eugene

"I think I found the thief," Supersonic Sal said.

"Little Miss Stinky Pinky!" Captain Awesome cried. "I should have seen your pink paws all over this caper!

"Would you *please* stop calling me that?! My name is Meredith, and this cupcake is mine!"

"Meredith," Ms. Beasley began in a calm voice. "Did you take that cupcake from someone else?"

"No! No! No! Ms. Beasley, I promise! This cupcake is mine! Mine! MINE!"

"*Meredith?*" the teacher asked again.

"Oh, okay, fine! I took it from Eu-germ." Meredith cracked like an egg on the side of a frying pan. "But then I was going to give it to Charlie. I double promise!"

"You were going to give it to me—I mean, *Charlie*?!" Nacho Cheese Man asked in disbelief.

"Now that the villain's been

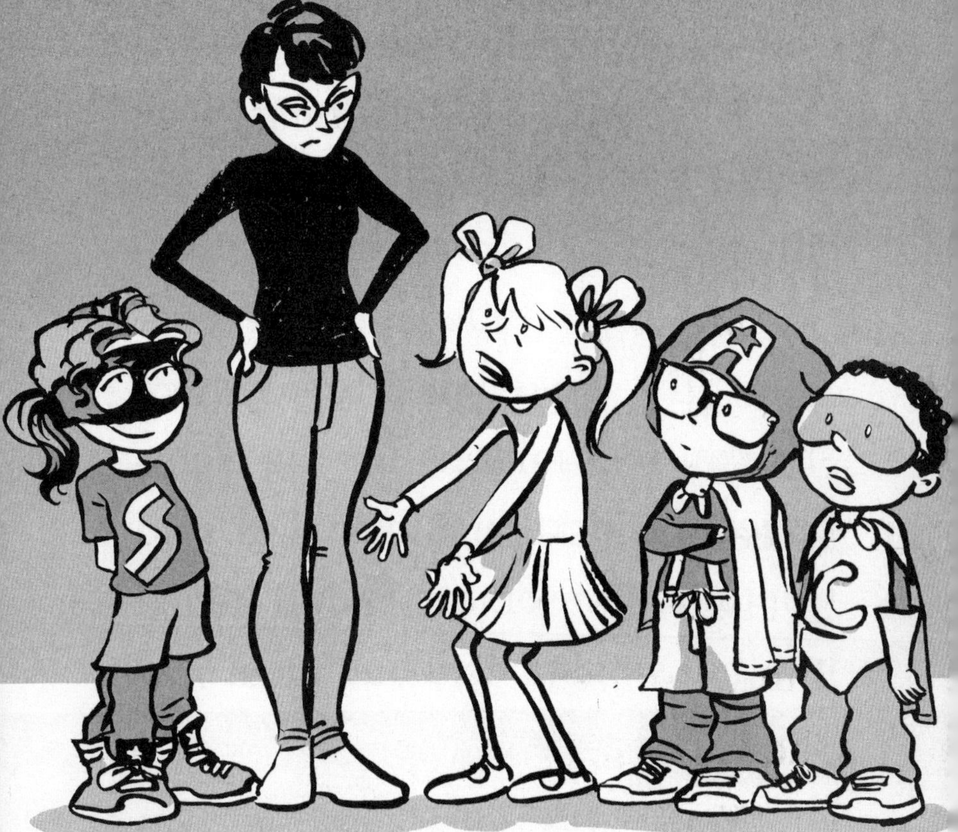

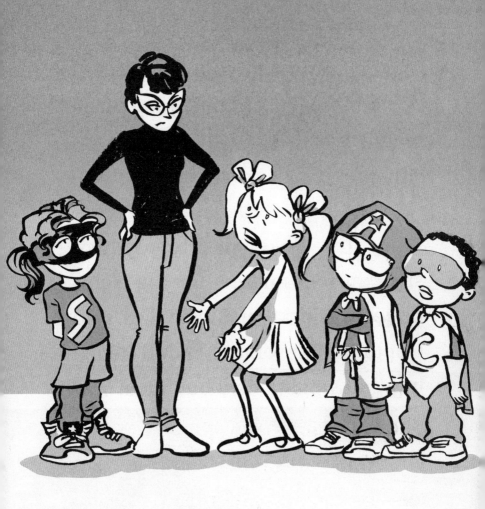

caught cupcake-handed, we need to send her to the Fortress of Evil-tude on the Planet Cake-battertopia where she can knit mittens for the eight-fingered Slorks of Slorkville," said Captain Awesome. "That'll teach her that stealing is a bad idea!"

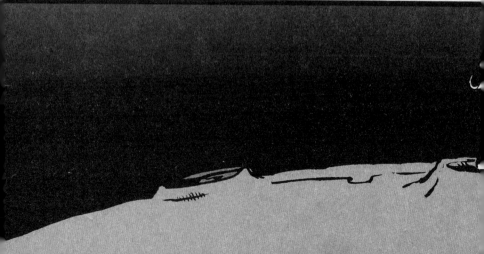

"Orrrr . . . we could forgive her," Nacho Cheese Man said in a voice so quiet that even *he* barely heard it.

"Yes," said Captain Awesome, agreeing. "We could

forgive her and—WHAT?! Did you say *forgive* her?!"

"Well, yeah, maybe. I mean, I'm just sayin'...,"Nacho Cheese Man mumbled.

"You better stop eating all that candy, Nacho Cheese Man,"replied Captain Awesome. "It's making you insane."

Then Nacho Cheese Man pulled

Captain Awesome and Supersonic Sal aside.

"She was going to give the cupcake to *me*," Nacho Cheese Man explained. "That's kind of cool."

"But she's a bad guy!" Captain Awesome protested. "And worse, she's a *pink* bad guy!"

All of a sudden, Supersonic Sal stepped between the two heroes. "Remember what Super Dude said in issue number 299 when he fought the League of Evil Babysitters? He said that to kick bad guy butt is super, but to forgive is heroic."

SHOCK!

"You're using Super Dude *against* me?! It's madness!" Captain Awesome cried in disbelief. But in his heart, he knew Sal—and Super Dude—were right. Sometimes the most heroic thing you can do . . . is just forgive.

"*Fine*," Captain Awesome said with a huff. He pointed his finger toward Nacho Cheese Man. "You owe me a cupcake!"

Nacho Cheese Man changed back into normal clothing, and then happily went to sit in his seat. Captain Awesome could only shake his head. "Valentine's Day does some pretty strange stuff to everyone. Good thing it only comes once a year."

"By the way, what did you get for Valentine's Day?" Supersonic Sal asked Captain Awesome.

"The greatest thing ever in the history of great things." Captain Awesome showed her his copy of *Super Dude Super Duper Spectacular Winter Extra Special* No. 1. "Whoever gave me this is a Super Dude fan . . . just like you!"

Supersonic Sal smiled. "Yep. Just like *me*," she said.

"Who do you think *your* secret admirer is?" Captain Awesome asked. "Not that I care. 'Cause I don't. Charlie cared. Not me."

Supersonic Sal looked over at Charlie, who was thoroughly enjoying the Missing Cupcake of Yumminess. He waved a "thank you" to Meredith. The only thing it looked like Charlie cared about was getting the perfect bite of cake *and* frosting. "Um, I don't really know who sent me the card," Supersonic Sal replied, then added a hopeful "I kinda thought it was . . . you?"

"Ha! Me? Well, I-I . . . ," Captain
Awesome stammered.

The two heroes shared an unex-
pected smile. Captain Awesome

suddenly felt an odd sensation in his cheeks. Was he . . . blushing?

"Better, um, change back into our secret identities before someone misses us," he said.

"Yeah, before someone misses us," Sal agreed.

Captain Awesome escaped to the cubbies, relieved this whole Valentine's Day thing was coming to an end. It was just too much crazy pinkness for one hero to handle.

Supersonic Sal watched as Captain Awesome disappeared

behind the cubbies, and then as Eugene came out and scurried to his seat.

"Well, happy Valentine's Day, Eugene," she said to herself and couldn't help but smile.

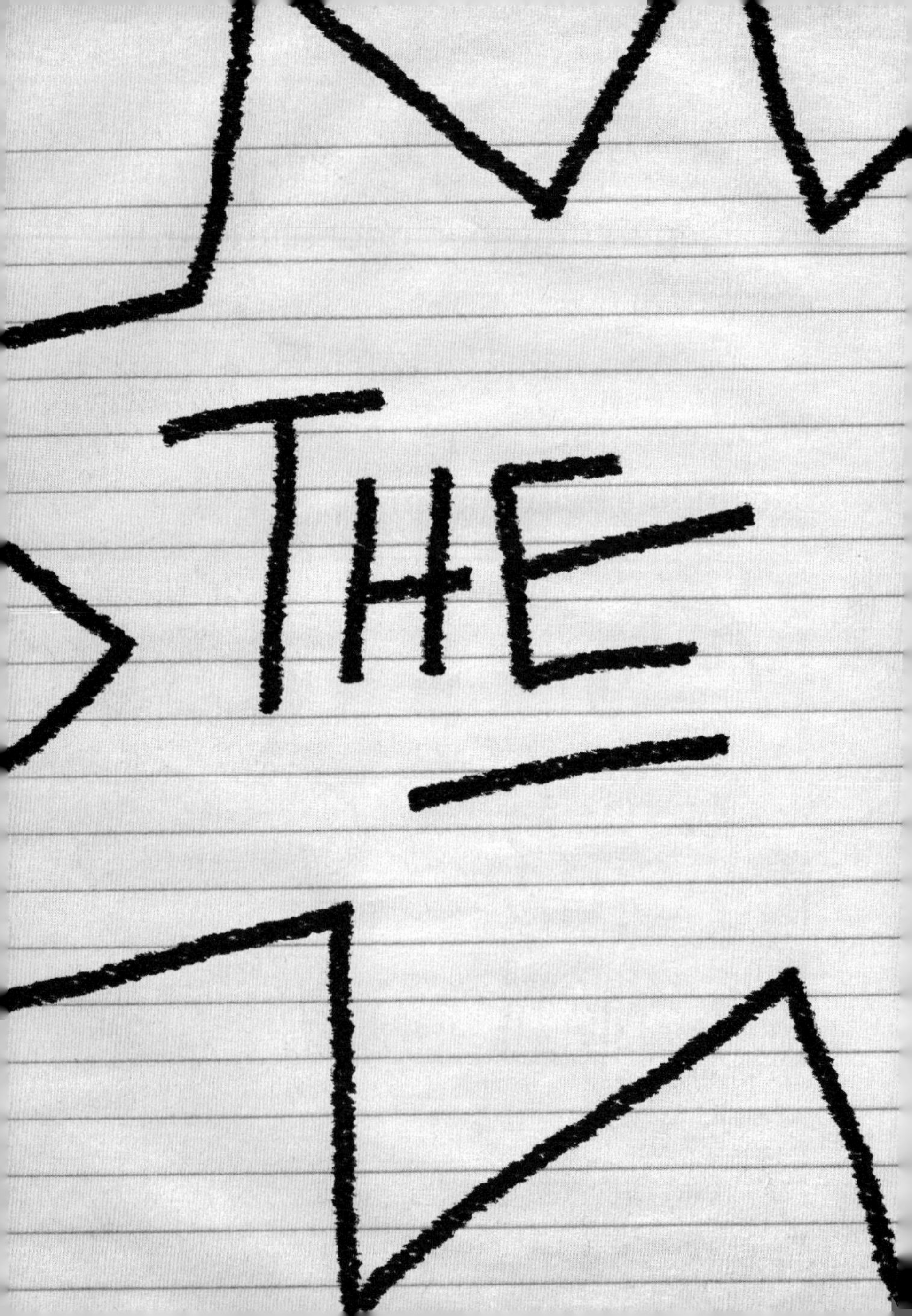
THE

END!

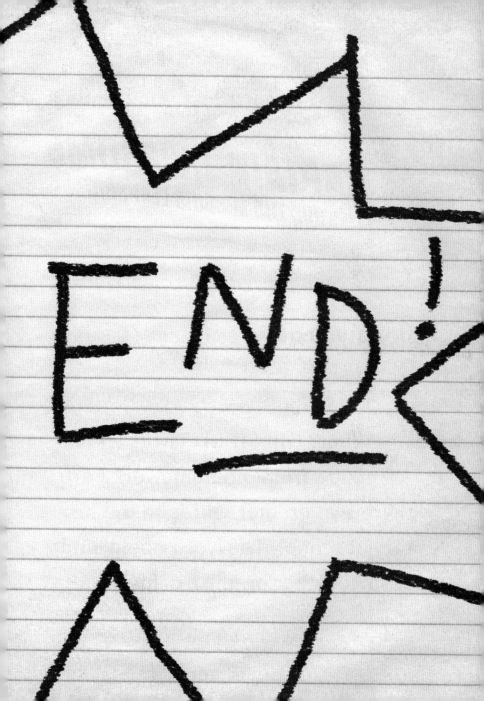

Keep reading for a sneak peek at the next Captain Awesome adventure!

CAPTAIN AWESOME
and the MISSING ELEPHANT

Two words:

FIELD!

TRIP!

What? Oh! FIELD TRIP!

Aside from "no homework," are there two greater words in the history of school? The words "field" and "trip" together promise a day of fun, a day away from school, and a day where anything can happen.

They're the chocolate and peanut butter of school.

And for Eugene, it was all going to happen tomorrow.

"Don't forget to bring your permission slips tomorrow, class," said Ms. Beasley, "or you won't be going to the zoo."

Eugene McGillicudy wouldn't miss a field trip any more than he'd miss New Comic Book Day at the comic book store.